THE WAY
OF THE LOON

A tale from the Boreal Forest

WRITTEN AND ILLUSTRATED
BY SALLY E. BURNS

Sally E. Burns

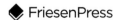 FriesenPress

Suite 300 - 990 Fort St
Victoria, BC, V8V 3K2
Canada

www.friesenpress.com

ISBN
978-1-5255-8244-8 (Hardcover)
978-1-5255-8245-5 (Paperback)
978-1-5255-8246-2 (eBook)

1. BJUVENILE FICTION, NATURE & THE NATURAL WORLD

Distributed to the trade by The Ingram Book Company

This book is for my granddaughter, Iris.

This is a book for adults to read aloud to children.

TABLE OF CONTENTS

ICE OUT

Winter was finally finished and waves lapped the shore once more. The ice was gone from the lake but in some places the wind had piled it up on the shore. Soon the dull hills would be touched with the clean, fresh green of leaves bursting forth on trees. Spring was here. Two small boys lay on their dock, staring down into the clear, cold water of the lake. They were trying to catch minnows in a dip net.

Two boys lay on their dock

The pair of loons flew over the boys

The younger boy said, "Here come some minnows; let me have a turn with the net."

His brother handed him the net and rolled onto his back just in time to see a pair of loons fly over. He knew loons when they flew by the way their feet stuck out behind them.

"Mom!" he called up to the house where their mother sat on the deck. "The loons are back."

"Yes, I see them too," she answered. Dapper and LaLa Loon flew right over the boys, crossing to the quiet side of the lake. They set their wings and glided in for a landing, dragging their feet in the water. *Swwwwwwiiisssh*, and down.

DANCING LOONS

Together again, LaLa, my dear," said Dapper. He stuck his head into the cold, clear water and took a good look around for food and then dove.

Dapper looked for food underwater

In an underwater hunt he found and ate a couple of the tasty little fish he liked. He resurfaced. "Oh yes, we are both at home here," he said happily. LaLa dove and hunted too. Finally, with their stomachs full, they cruised around happily on the lake. The breeze died and dusk fell. "Yes, it is good to be back again," said LaLa.

The mood was right for loon romance. The two loons swam toward each other, rapidly dipping their bills in the water and then flipping them out again.

They did a couple of short dives together. They reared up side by side, beat their wings and paddled their feet, running across the water in a straight line, while giving their tremolo loon calls.

Then they turned around and did this same dance right back to their starting spot. They thought they looked splendid!

They settled on the water again and looked at each other contentedly. They were very happy together.

They danced together across the water

So Many Lakes

Across the lake at the house, the boys were in their beds. Their mom kissed them goodnight and turned out their lights. She was leaving when the younger boy said, "The loons must like our lake. They come back here every year."

"Yes," agreed their mother. "They and all loons before them have been coming back to these lakes for years and years and years, since the big glaciers melted. Every year, when winter ice melts, they come back to nest and have a family, eat fish from these clear, clean lakes, and call and laugh to the hills around their lake of choice. Listen tonight and you may hear them."

She left their room, leaving the door open a crack. The children were asleep before she was down the stairs. In the middle of the night, in the middle of the lake, Dapper and LaLa Loon swam side by side. Dapper yodelled out his own special call to tell other loons this was their chosen place and he and LaLa were going to nest here.

DAPPER CHOOSES A NESTING SPOT

As the days warmed up Dapper and LaLa swam the shoreline together. "I'm not nesting where Old Hungry and Talon can watch me again," LaLa said firmly. That was the pair of eagles who had robbed them of their babies the last summer.

"No, dear," Dapper agreed. "This is our nesting lake now. We know where Old Hungry watches from and we'll find a secret spot, away from his eagle eye." He steered LaLa towards a point on the shore with a tiny rock islet just off its end.

"I think this is the place," he said. "I'll tuck the nest up in amongst the sweet-smelling bushes, at the top of that sloping rock." LaLa cocked her head, thought about it and then agreed.

"No animals can sneak up on me there," she said happily, "and the eagles have their nest in a different bay on the lake."

She cruised slowly, nearby, while Dapper waddled ashore and worked on a simple nest. He pulled together dead grass and reeds washed up on the shoreline. He tucked these into a cozy opening in the low, sweet-smelling bushes. For his finishing touch he sank into the simple nest and made a comfy depression in it for LaLa. Then he called her up to see it.

She was very pleased and they snuggled happily for a bit, close to the nest up on the little island.

"Now, LaLa," Dapper said as LaLa nestled down in the depression in the nest, "make some of those big, brown, beautiful speckled eggs."

"That is my plan, Dapper, dear," she answered happily and settled down to concentrate on egg laying.

BIG, BROWN, BEAUTIFUL SPECKLED EGGS

After snuggling with Dapper and settling into her new nest, LaLa thought good thoughts about big, brown, beautiful speckled eggs: how she would form them in her body and lay them in her nest. She and Dapper would take turns sitting on them, turning them, guarding them, keeping them warm and hatching them.

Before long she laid two eggs in her nest. They were lovely and perfect and "a sight to behold," as Dapper said when LaLa showed them to him. He was very proud of his beautiful lady loon and her amazing eggs.

LaLa was tired from the effort of producing them.

"Now I will rest and doze," she said.

"Think good thoughts, LaLa, my love," Dapper called as he paddled away. "If I give my eagle yelp, do not move even one feather, for it will mean Old Hungry is about. I'll come and take my turn when you call."

"Keep good watch, Dapper dear, but not too close to me or you'll give us away," answered LaLa as she settled in for her first turn of the long wait.

LaLa settled in for her long wait

That night the hills echoed with Dapper's happy yodel calls. LaLa enjoyed the concert. Only he could give the particular call she liked so well.

"A-a-whee-quee-quee-whe ooo quee."

In their beds in the house, the little boys stirred, listening in the dark to the loon concert.

WATCHING INVISIBLY, WAITING PATIENTLY

One day, after Dapper had taken his turn on the nest and LaLa was now keeping the eggs warm, a canoe came into view, gliding along the shore close to the nest. The paddlers were fishing with a rod stuck out the back of the canoe. A medium-size dog lay on top of their packs in the middle of the canoe. Then the man in the back grabbed the rod.

LaLa watched as they landed a flashing and splashing lake trout. Next, the fishermen with the dog pulled up on a large flat rock down the shore from her nesting islet. She watched, but did not twitch a feather. The dog ran around sniffing and exploring. LaLa had to keep from shuddering. Almost as bad as a fox, she thought.

Then Dapper gave his little warning hoot and her blood froze in her veins. She became so still she seemed not to breathe. Old Hungry or Talon had been spotted and must not see her, or those eagles would watch them on the nest and steal the chicks when they hatched.

Old Hungry and his mate, Talon, would eat fish in any form. Fish guts, heads, and skin would do for them and their family. Old Hungry watched the people on the shore. He had spied the silvery flash of the trout as it fought its last fight beside the canoe. He drifted in and landed in a nearby pine tree. He watched and waited while the fish were cleaned. Far above, Talon circled unseen.

Far above, Talon circled, unseen

Down the shore, Dapper watched Old Hungry land in the pine tree not far from the canoers. That eagle sees a lot from a long way off, Dapper grudgingly admitted. Old Hungry has spotted the fish. Dapper hooted his little warning to LaLa. It was a quick, single-noted "hooo." It was quiet, but it carried.

The fish cleaned, the paddlers tucked their trout supper into a bag, pushed off, dog and all, leaving the fish remains on the flat rock shore.

The minute the canoe left two crows landed by the fish guts. Old Hungry dropped off his perch and glided in for a landing, near the fish. Then came Talon, Old Hungry's hard-eyed mate, swooping in like a fighter jet. The crows made off in a hurry, cawing in outrage and bitter disappointment at losing their easy meal. Talon seized one set of fish remains and flapped off to her nest and hungry young ones with fish skins trailing behind her like the tail of a kite.

She knows how to get the job done, thought LaLa as she stared motionless from the nest. It's a good thing those fishermen distracted them. I believe our nest is still undiscovered. Dapper stayed well away and warned me. Really though, she sniffed, some birds will eat anything. I like my fish small, whole and still wriggling, not somebody else's leftovers.

Old Hungry pecked at the loose bits of lake trout fins and ribs to grab a quick bite before he carried the rest of the remains off to feed his babies.

They have hungry young ones growing fast, Dapper thought. We must be sure they don't spot our nest site like they did last year!

With both eagles gone, Dapper cruised back to the nest site where LaLa sat. He gave her the "all clear" nod. He waddled up the rock to take his turn on the nest as she slid down the rock and entered the water without a ripple.

LaLa caught a few small fish to ease her hunger. She fished and fed for a while and bathed and preened. She splashed and rolled in the water. With her bill she nosed at a place at the base of her tail where the oil for preening her feathers was stored.

"I must get back to my sitting soon but taking care of my feathers is important too," she told herself.

She worked the oil into the wing feathers, rolled onto one side and with one leg waving in the air, preened her white breast feathers.

Then, satisfied with her grooming, she rose up and flapped her wings. She dove smoothly, surfacing beside the nesting spot and shot out of the water onto the shore. Clumsily, she waddled to her nest.

"I'm not built for walking," she muttered as she waddled her way back into position over her eggs and Dapper slid into the water. "My legs are so far back on my body that walking is an awkward business. In the water I can turn and seek and dodge to catch my darting dinner."

She tucked some more reeds from the shore-line into the nest and with her bill slightly open she turned the eggs. She did this regularly to keep the eggs heated evenly.

"Now for some more sitting," she said and settled on the nest.

LaLa turned her eggs

THE HATCH

The days went by. The loon couple sat patiently through rain and sun, storm and wind, taking turns keeping the eggs warm. On the twenty-ninth day Dapper was off on a fishing foray out in a deeper part of the lake.

LaLa was thinking happy thoughts on her nest when she was interrupted by a tapping sound coming from an egg.

"Oh my, oh my, it's happening!" she gasped.

She shifted her weight off that egg. Finally, there was a crack and the egg broke open wide.

Out came a little chick, who peeked all around and sat drying in the sun, amongst the pieces of shell. The chick was peeping and chirring and it sounded like wee, giggling chortles. LaLa listened to him and decided his name. "We'll call you Chortle, my little one," she told him.

When he was dry, he nestled into LaLa's feathers, with just his head peeking out. LaLa happily and proudly tucked him in and waited for the second egg to hatch.

Out came a little chick

Nothing happened. Then Dapper came winging in, and landed in front of her. "Well, well," he said. "Mother LaLa! Look at you with a pretty little sooty-coloured chick."

LaLa nodded proudly as a queen. "Meet your son, Chortle," she said happily. "Take a turn on this other egg please, Dapper. Chortle and I are going for a swim."

She waddled to the water's edge with Chortle right behind. He paddled in the water for about three seconds. Then, with help from LaLa, who sank herself lower in the water, he scrambled onto her tail and up onto her back. The water was cold for such a little fellow. His downy feathers were not like LaLa's well-oiled, waterproof ones. LaLa sailed out from the nest site and cruised along the shore with her baby on board.

LaLa with Chortle on her back

That summer night LaLa sat back on the nest with little Chortle tucked in, asleep. She was still waiting for the second egg to hatch.

The darkness echoed with Dapper's happy calls. He yodelled and declared his territory to all others with his "a-a-whee-quee-quee-whe ooo quee" call, repeated several times.

LaLa thought Dapper's yodel was the best she had ever heard.

LaLa waited in vain for another day for the second egg to hatch, but it did not hatch and the loons abandoned the nest. It was disappointing, but there was too much to do feeding the baby who had hatched. She remembered a passing motorboat that had pushed big, cold waves up the shore, partially swamping the nest and probably chilling that egg. It was time to move on.

LaLa waited another day for the second egg to hatch

The following days were busy ones for both parents, catching small snails and leeches to feed their baby.

Now, they moved to a sandy shallow bay where they could easily feed Chortle. It had a gradual drop off to deep water and they could find different food at different depths.

Soon Chortle could take small fish and both parents delivered them to him, eating some too when they had a chance. At night, Chortle would still climb on LaLa's back for a warm, dry roost. But more and more he was swimming beside whichever parent was not diving. He would stick his head underwater and look down, and bob under, imitating his parents. He could rear up and stretch his little wings like they did. His down turned from sooty black to a lighter brown. He was growing and changing with each minnow he gulped down.

His parents took turns feeding Chortle

THE CLOSE CALL

It was an overcast day with a breeze. The loon family was in an open part of the lake. As usual, LaLa and Dapper were taking turns feeding Chortle. There was a large dead fish, floating belly up nearby. It was not of interest to the loons, for as Dapper liked to say, "Loons like their fish fresh and frisky," and much smaller than that dead one.

Chortle was growing up with brown and white feathers now replacing his down. For the third day in a row Dapper was telling Chortle he should really try diving down deep and hunting his own food.

"Chort, my boy, you have to give it a try. There's nothing like the thrill of the chase in an underwater pursuit. To dive deep, tuck your head down and curl your back up to follow your head, and down you go with a flip of your feet."

Chortle opened his bill and gulped down what LaLa had brought him. Dapper sighed and looked around before his next dive.

Looking for fish

Suddenly there was a rush of wings and a big black and white shape streaking in from above.

"Dive!" squawked Dapper as he reared up on his tail and flapped his wings, bravely facing the incoming eagle.

Dapper reared up bravely

LaLa turned to Chortle, but with Dapper's instructions still fresh in his mind, Chortle tucked and dove right down, and LaLa did too, just as the large black and white shape shot over them, legs outstretched ahead of her, reaching for her target.

Talon rocketed over them reaching for her target

Talon grabbed the dead fish

Chortle popped back to the surface in time to see Talon, the mother eagle, seize the floating, dead fish while still remaining airborne.

LaLa gasped. "That was close!"

Talon flapping away with the dead fish

Chortle just sputtered. Dapper watched in awe as Talon flapped heavily away, struggling to lift high enough to carry her large load back to her nest.

"Those eagle babies must be getting very large," said LaLa. "Do you think she was after Chortle?"

"The fish is bigger," Dapper said shortly, as he watched Talon disappear in the direction of her nest. "Fortunately, Chort dove fast and deep as soon as I yelled 'dive'... Well done, my son!"

Chortle was pleased with the praise and threw himself underwater again. It was another world down there and he took a good look around. This diving and hunting could be fun, he thought.

After the sun had set and the stars were glowing in the black sky, Dapper and LaLa called happily back and forth to each other. Chortle felt the whole world was pleased with his accomplishment.

"A hoo looooo looooo," Dapper wailed.

LaLa called back with a "Laaaa Laaaa la ha ha ha" in the tremolo.

Then Dapper gave his high nasal yodel, his special male loon call. It was a show stopper! Chortle tried to imitate it but Dapper laughed and told him, "You don't have the pipes yet, my boy. Start with the simple wailing call first."

Chort gave an "ahaa-ooo-oooo."

"Not bad," his father said approvingly.

The loon family called on the lake at night

THE BUG-EYED BONEHEADS

Chortle grew bigger and stronger every day. In his new feathers he was starting to look like a loon, not a ball of fluff. He was diving and catching his own fish. He found he liked smelts, another kind of small fish which lived in the lake. He was learning fancy underwater moves. One of these meant he could change direction quickly when chasing small fish.

Dapper showed him how to
turn fast underwater

33

Swimming fast, he would thrust one leg out to the side, and with the other leg still kicking hard, he could turn sharply. Dapper had shown him this.

His parents worried because he wasn't even thinking about flying yet, and he did not swim long distances underwater.

It was a hot, sleepy summer day but there were some cottages on the lake and the cottagers were active. Dapper found some people harmless. However, some had jet skis and at times they roared around on them endlessly and aimlessly, sometimes harassing birds and animals. Dapper disliked these people on the machines intensely and had his own name for them and their riders, who often wore buggy-eyed sunglasses. To Dapper they were the Bug-Eyed Boneheads.

The loon family was basking, preening, and bathing in the middle of the lake when all at once, the lazy calm of the summer's day was broken by the roar of two flashy jet skis racing across the surface. They were aiming straight at the loons.

"It's the Bug-Eyed Boneheads," said Dapper with some alarm as he turned an angry red eye towards one of the droning beasts. "Sink down and see if they'll buzz by us." The loons squeezed their feathers tight, forcing air out, and semi-submerged.

The loon family squeezed their feathers tight and rode low in the water

But the creatures on the howling machines were not deceived. They drew ever closer, pointing at the loons and screaming at each other.

"It's the real idiots this time. Take evasive action!" Dapper commanded.

Dapper, LaLa, and Chortle dove. The Bug-Eyed Boneheads blasted right over where the birds had been sitting. Chortle watched the bubbles above him as they roared by.

It's okay to surface now, he thought. They've gone.

He popped up and was looking around for his parents when he realized the Bug-Eyed Boneheads had spun around and were coming at him again. He dove again in a hurry and travelled a little distance. He had no idea where his parents were.

Again, he popped up. He stared, aghast. The Bug-Eyed Boneheads had spun and were practically on him.

They circled him in ever-tighter circles, causing rocking, rough waves to come at him from all directions, bouncing him madly about. He was surrounded by the howling, circling beasts. His heart was pounding and he wanted his mom!

Chortle alone by the island

In gaps between the circling machines he spotted the island. He heard his father's voice in his head telling him "the best way to disappear on the surface of the lake is to dive and surface close in tight against a shore."

Get to that shore! he told himself.

He tucked and dove about ten feet down. He sped toward the island, working his feet hard to race away, leaving the howl of the Bug-Eyed Boneheads in the distance.

When he saw the bottom of the lake below him, sloping up to the island's shoreline, he surfaced tight against the shore and swam quickly around to the other side of the island.

"Safe from the Bug-Eyed Boneheads, but alone for the first time in my life," he said aloud.

He peered into the trees on the shore, and listened to the very distant drone of the Bug-Eyed Boneheads, who had roared away to a far shore when Chort disappeared.

HE'S GONE

Chortle's parents surfaced and stared at the place where he had been corralled by the circling machines. All they saw was empty, frothy water.

"He just didn't have a chance," sobbed LaLa. "Last year it was the eagles. Now this!"

"I fear the worst, but we must not give up. We must look," Dapper spoke solemnly.

They craned their necks in every direction. They peered and dove and looked underwater. LaLa was giving little sad, one note hoot calls.

"La? Hoo?… Hooo? La…"

Dapper sat still now and muttered, "He listens to me. Chort knows in order to escape, dive or fly… but he can't fly… maybe he dove and swam… if he could even think with that ruckus and racket so close to him… I must find him. LaLa is so upset, she is not thinking clearly. I must think. If he dove, where would he go? We can't see him. I have told him: to hide on a calm lake, get against a shore. The nearest shore is that island."

He looked at LaLa, who was looking very lost and sad.

"LaLa, dear, I have an idea! Maybe he dove and swam to that island to escape and disappear."

"Never that far," said LaLa hopelessly.

"I must look," said Dapper with resolve.

"I'll stay here in case he comes back from underwater," LaLa said, sticking her head underwater yet again.

Dapper took off and rose for a good view. He could see no other birds on the water. He circled the island, calling. Suddenly, below him, in close to the island, he saw Chortle, who reared up and flapped his little wings. Dapper swung around and down and swished to a stop beside his son.

"My boy! How did you get here? We thought you were gone. Your mother is in despair."

Chortle hiccupped with the relief and pleasure of his dad finding him.

"Dad, I saw the island between the circling beasts. I could hear your voice advising me 'to escape, fly or dive… when on the water, get close to land to be unseen from a distance.' So, I did!"

"Chortle, my son, I am so happy and relieved and proud you escaped. Now I must go quickly and bring your mother. Stay here."

Dapper took off and was back immediately with LaLa, who lavished Chortle with all her attention and a relieved mother's love.

"That entire way underwater, Chortle! You are truly a great northern diver. Now let's get over deeper water. These shallows can be dangerous too."

That night in the full moon Dapper serenaded his family and the summer night echoed with his yodels. LaLa joined in with some tremolo laughs and Chortle tried a few wails himself, feeling safe, happy, and proud, all at once.

Do others listening think this as awesome as I do? he wondered.

~

In their beds the children woke and heard the loons calling and fell asleep again knowing all was well in their world.

MISTER SAW JAWS

Some days later, Dapper, LaLa, and Chortle were all diving and feeding. Chortle was getting closer to shore than LaLa liked, but in the shallows were small fish he liked to eat. He found them easy to catch. On one of his dives close to shore he was startled to see a very long, large fish lying in the water, perfectly still, just above the bottom alongside a sunken log. The log helped camouflage him.

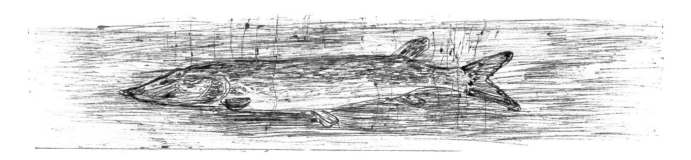

Mister Saw Jaws the Northern Pike

There was something about the huge fish and the way it silently eyed him that Chortle did not trust, but he slowed for a better look. A few small bass swam into view, unaware of the danger behind the log. But the big fish was fanning his fins and turning toward the bass and the little loon. Slowly, slowly, danger turned and stared at the little loon.

With a sudden thrust of his powerful tail, the big fish shot forward and with jaws agape he swallowed an unsuspecting bass in the wink of an eye! The monster fish swallowed hard again, then sank back down, turning now to eye the little loon once more.

Terrified, Chortle was off like a shot, spinning hard, and heading fast for deep water where he had last seen LaLa. He surfaced beside her.

"Mom! Big fish! Ate bass whole!" he blurted out.

"Just what I meant when I said the shallows can be dangerous too," said LaLa sharply.

Dapper surfaced beside them and listened with a serious look.

"Who is he?" asked Chortle.

"He is Saw Jaws the Northern Pike. You must stay as far away from him as you can. He could come after you in a flash and swallow you whole. We wouldn't even know what had happened to you," said Dapper sternly.

"I was watching him too," said Chortle. "I think he was lining me up for his next mouthful."

"You are lucky that bass swam into the ambush," said Dapper. "You saw what Saw Jaws can do. His huge mouth with rows of sharp teeth could swallow you whole."

"What does he eat?" asked Chortle, horrified but fascinated.

Laffsalot had two chicks

"Everything and anyone who looks small enough to swallow, and that covers a lot, so stay far away from him. You always want to see him coming before he sees you."

"My sister, Laffsalot, had two chicks one year," added LaLa. "She lost one, a little smaller than you. They were at the entrance to a shallow bay. There was a swirling surge of water rising from below, an eruption on the surface, and Chickie was gone, never to be seen again."

44

"It isn't only loon babies Saw Jaws will grab," continued LaLa. "You've noticed Mrs. Rustyhead, the duck, with her straggling brood of babies. I'm sure that duck can't count or she'd be crying every day. She started with twelve ducklings. They always cruise the shallows. She's down to eight now. She has lost four so far."

"Has Saw Jaws eaten them all?" gasped Chortle in horror.

"Either that or Old Hungry or Talon nabbed one or two," said Dapper.

"How big will Saw Jaws get?"

"From the air, in the spring, I've seen some very large pike in the creek flowing from this lake. They were there to lay their eggs when I first returned, before your mother arrived. They were large pike, very large pike…"

Chortle was silent for a bit, thinking about Chickie, his lost cousin and the huge fish with the appetite to match, and the wide, saw toothed jaws.

"Dad," he asked "Do you think there's a pike big enough to devour you?

"Perhaps, perhaps," said Dapper.

"What about a muskrat like the one we saw coming out of the creek the other day?"

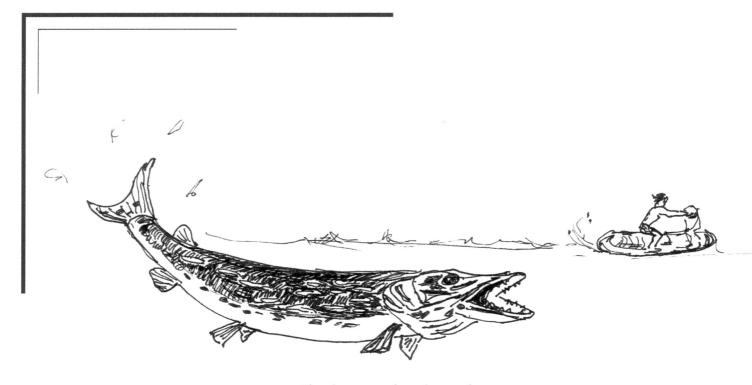

*Chortle imagined a Pike attack on
the Bug-Eyed Boneheads*

"Well maybe, a small muskrat and a very large pike, if the pike came up from below, out of the depths and dragged him down."

"What about a Bug-Eyed Bonehead?" giggled Chortle and pictured it with glee.

"Well, you never know, but watch what you wish for, my boy!" his father said laughing when he pictured that idea.

Storm

The days of summer were sliding by. Some were still, sunny, and hot, some cloudy and cooler. Some started clear and clouds blew in by afternoon. This day was very hot. Dapper would occasionally shake a foot in the air behind him to cool off.

The air felt heavy and thick. It barely stirred, until finally a huge wall of billowing cloud loomed in the west.

A huge wall of billowing cloud moved in from the west

Then there was a sudden little breeze and riffles ran across the lake

In a higher voice than usual Dapper announced, "We're in for a boomer," and without another word ran across the surface, took off, and flew around the lake calling wildly and disappeared.

Chortle sat staring after him with questions on his mind about "boomers": what were they, and where had his father gone in such a hurried manner?

LaLa faced the far shore and said quite briskly, "Right then! With a thunderstorm coming we are headed to a sheltered shore, out of the wind. Your father is off announcing bad weather."

She swam off, leading the way with purpose.

"Come, Chortle," she said. "In this you must listen to me. You need to be in the right spot when this kind of storm arrives. I hate to say it, but thunderstorms make your father crazy. Or some would say 'loonie,'" she muttered under her breath.

She led him to a steep, wooded shoreline, out of the wind, overhung by cedars growing by the shore. The gathering storm had the wind howling above the trees but LaLa and Chortle were in a calm place.

All at once there was a flash, a crack, and a boom, right across the bay from them.

Chortle stood up on his tail and flapped his little wings with fright. Lightning had struck a tall pine across the bay, blowing the top to pieces. Bits of the tree now floated in the water. Chortle was wide-eyed and silent. Maybe that was why thunderstorms upset his dad.

Then rain fell so hard and heavily that drops bounced off the water. Chortle could not see through the downpour. There were more flashes and booms, but none as loud as the first. None of this bothered LaLa, who seemed to enjoy the downpour when the booms and flashes weren't so close. Chortle was still on edge from the first lightning strike. He paddled up close to his mom.

"It's not a good idea to be out in the middle of the lake when the lightning comes," LaLa said after the rain had eased and the thunder only boomed in the distance. "Where it will choose to land and roar is a mystery. A low shoreline like this one seems safe to me."

"Where's Dad?" asked Chortle.

"He's nervous," LaLa said shortly. "He probably flew off to avoid the whole thing. He'll be back soon. Announcing the storm to everyone calms him."

Sure enough, Dapper flew in, cruising to a landing beside them without a word about where he had been, or why he had left. He put on a show for them, rearing up and dancing across the water, wings spread, sitting back on his tail. LaLa was very taken by it and cocked her head to one side, entranced.

"Parents!" said Chortle and he stuck his head underwater. "Sometimes you just have to guess what's going on," he grumbled. "He flies off without a word. Then he comes back and shows off."

Cooling off

Voices On the Breeze

One morning their lake was shrouded in a grey mist. The rising sun's first rays touched the mist, turning it pink. Slowly, the mist swirled, rose, thinned and drifted away.

Chortle was very interested.

"What was that stuff and why was it hiding the island?" he asked.

"It's mist. It's a sign, a kind of notice. It comes when the days shorten and nights cool," Dapper told him.

"It means autumn, or the fall season, is coming," LaLa added.

Chortle, of course, had more questions:

"What is fall? I hear the voices on the breeze talking in the early morning. They too say, 'fall is coming… fall is coming.'"

"It's good you are in tune with the voices on the wind. They will warn you the seasons are changing," said LaLa.

"What are the seasons and why does it matter if I hear the breeze talking about fall coming?" wondered Chortle aloud.

LaLa explained, as she always did. "Since you hatched, there have been long, warm sunny days."

"And some rainy ones," reminded Chortle.

"Yes."

"And thunderstorms."

"Yes. And they are all part of spring, summer, and early fall seasons."

"Seasons?"

"Oh, so much explaining," sighed LaLa. She went on. "Seasons are the four different parts of the year: spring, summer, fall, and winter. It is important to pay attention and notice changes in the seasons. In spring your father and I return from the south where we have been for fall and winter. We come back here to nest and raise our chicks. In late spring or early summer, loon chicks hatch out of their eggs and begin to grow and learn, and ask questions, it seems," she said with a smile in her voice. "Through summer we raise our chicks, eat the clean food of these northern lakes, sing, and laugh. In fall, the sun comes up later and goes down sooner. Days become shorter and nights longer. The sun is lower across the sky and barely warms us or the water. Lakes cool and mists form. With winter coming, we all fly away to where we can play happily on ocean waters or big lakes with no ice, to escape the hard bite of winter."

"The bite of winter?" asked Chortle.

"Winter is a cold and cruel time. These lakes become icy cold and freeze, hard as a rock shore, all across the surface. Loons cannot swim on frozen lakes. Rain turns to snow, which is white. It sticks on trees and piles up on the ground. We loons must leave and follow the sun as it dips south in the sky."

"But I like it here," protested Chort, who was still not flying and had not shown much interest in trying to learn.

"Your father and I like it here too," agreed LaLa, "but not in winter. We cannot live on frozen lakes. Your father will leave first, then I will follow, but only when I know you can manage on your own. You will stay here until you are ready for the trip. Then you will fly south too."

Chortle was quiet for a few moments. Then he said, "I think I should practice my take-off skills."

"Finally!" breathed LaLa.

TAKING OFF

"W atch your father when he goes," LaLa called to Chortle. She was teaching him how to take off for flight. "He leans forward, flaps, kicks his feet underwater to get up on top of the surface, and begins to run across it. Practice that."

Chortle flapped his wings and rose up a bit.

LaLa urged him on. "And now, kick those feet as if you were going to dive underwater. But don't dive, just lean forward, stretch your neck out and look straight ahead. Flap your wings and start running."

"That's a lot to remember," muttered Chortle.

"Just do it!" said his mother. "Every loon who lives learns to do this."

He flapped and kicked and only raised himself up a little.

"Lean forward as you do that. Look where you want to go," urged his mother.

He kicked, he flapped, he leaned forward, and he looked down the lake. Lo and behold, he was up and running across the water!

"Keep going, keep flapping and running. Stretch your neck out!"

He stopped and paddled back. "I went quite a way," he said.

"Flap harder and just keep running," insisted LaLa.

It was Chortle's turn to sigh. "It's hard," he moaned.

Dapper had just landed near them.

"Come on, Chort, my boy," he said, "right beside me."

Off they went, big, heavy, strong, black and white Dapper running and flapping, and little brown and white Chortle, giving it everything he had. He was up and running. He was flapping and running and watching his dad ahead of him, and, finally, he was off the water and flying!

He was up: it was easier when free of the water. The air was under his wings. His dad was beside him and they were both flying. He loved it! It was as if he had always done it.

They rounded the island and came back over LaLa who rose up on her tail and called to them in

They flew together in a row

excitement. Dapper called back and she ran across the water and joined them in the air.

They flew all around the lake, Dapper leading the way, calling out happily. Then he led them in for a landing.

"Uh-oh, here goes," said Chortle, his heart pounding in fear. "This may not be pretty. I have no idea how to do this."

He followed his father, watching him closely. They came in low, and lower. Then Dapper was dragging his feet across the water, keeping his head up until his chest sank and plowed through the water. Chortle followed him exactly, and landed. LaLa was right behind. All three were sitting on the lake again.

"Wow! Let's do it again!" said Chortle.

It all came quite easily after that. Chort knew he could not yet fly as far as his parents, but it was something he was more than happy to practice. His parents made sure he flew farther and longer each day, but that was not hard to do. He loved flying!

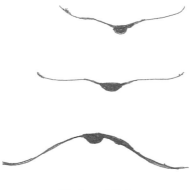

He loved flying.

Shorter Days, Sparkling Water

"Look how the water sparkles golden now," noticed Chortle one day.

"Yes," agreed LaLa. "Soon we must chase the sun south."

"So that we aren't here when the water turns hard as rock?"

"That's right. First the air and water turn colder and then very cold. Promise me you won't stay for the very cold."

"I won't," promised Chortle. It didn't sound like they would be leaving together. That was scary.

LaLa noticed his look. "You will be fine, my son. You know how to swim, fish, fly, and land, and to spot danger and flee."

"But I don't know where to go," Chortle sighed.

His mother tried to reassure him. "Relax and believe. Those little voices on the breeze will tell you it's time to leave and the pull in your heart will guide you on your journey."

"Good to know," muttered Chortle glumly.

Dapper's
Departure

Every day Chortle flew a little farther than the last day. He knew he must get bigger and stronger to fly away, to make the big trip south. All by himself. In the air he could see the world stretch out in all directions. The higher he went, the farther he could see. He learned so much when he flew. It was such a different view from when he sat on the water, or when he swam underwater to catch his fishy meals.

When he swam underwater there was a purpose: to find food or escape danger. Underwater was darker but his good red eyes saw well. He swam fast and nabbed his meals whenever he was hungry. The deeper he went, the darker it got, but usually the small fish he ate were travelling in schools, well above the bottom. He ate his fill when he found them.

When he sat on the surface he could swim around or rest and watch his parents, or other birds. The other birds were starting to gather and talk amongst themselves about the migration south. There were even some geese beginning to fly over in lines, gabbling away about getting in shape for the big journey. There was a lot to be seen from the water too.

But when he flew, oh my, what a big world it was! The lakes below him all became choices of places he could land. Dapper occasionally mentioned to little Chortle a mighty river to follow in migration, right to the Big Salt Gulf.

"Follow it from the sky, my son," he said. "It is brown water all the way to the Big Salt Gulf. You can't dive in that river and find any food. Even resting on it is not a good idea. Get a few dozen bellyfuls of fish before you leave lake country. That food will have to see you through a good distance. Then find more lakes for resting and eating partway through the trip."

The journey south! Chortle got worried when he thought about it. But then he decided all he could do was prepare. He would eat, grow, fly, and be strong for the journey.

One morning Dapper was quite restless. Chortle could see it. Dapper did a few short dives and popped up beside LaLa and Chortle.

"Well, I'm on my way," he said. "See you here next spring, LaLa, my dear."

"What about seeing me too?" Chortle asked, upset at being left out.

"Oh, you won't head back up here until you are two or three years old. Once you are down in the Big Salt Gulf you will grow big and strong like me, with black and white feathers like mine. You will go north with other young loons to spend summers on lakes with lots of food. When you are all grown up you will come north to a lovely lake like this one. You will find a pretty loon lady (as smart and beautiful as your mother,) to make a nest for, and to snuggle with, and raise chicks; but not for a while yet… not for a couple of years. In the meantime, grow strong, fly south, and prosper, Chortle, my son. You know I am proud of you. I've tried to teach and protect you as best I can. I believe you can make your way in the world. You are a good, smart, strong, little loon. I hope we'll meet again. The voices on the breeze are getting quite loud and so leave I must! I'm off!"

"Funny, I can't hear them," said Chortle.

But Dapper did not dilly-dally with more talk. He was gone, running across the lake until he flew. He circled them, called twice and was gone.

"I don't believe it," said Chortle. "He just left us."

"Believe it," said his mother gently. "We are loons and that is the way of the loon."

He was gone, running across the lake until he flew

"Tell me where I'm supposed to go after you leave me all by myself," insisted Chortle, watching his mother closely to make sure she was not getting restless too.

"I'll try, but it isn't a matter for telling. You just do it. Listen for the voices on the wind to guide you along the way and learn as you go. Wait for the pull in your chest and heed it."

LaLa Leaves

After a few days, Chortle was tired of wondering how he would find his way to the Big Salt Gulf. He started asking his mother again.

"All right," she said. "Here is all I can tell you about when it's time for you to go. First, you face the sun in the morning. If there are voices on the breeze saying 'Go now! Go now!' you take off and fly with the sun on your sunrise side. Then, by afternoon, the sun will have moved across in front of you and you will keep it on your sunset side. You will feel a pull in the right direction if you keep your mind quiet and pay attention. So, pay attention! If fierce winds blow you off your course, sit down on water and wait for better weather.

"When you leave, you will fly over one long narrow lake stretching out in the direction of sunrise to sunset. This will be followed by many small and medium-sized lakes. You can land and rest on lakes big enough for a takeoff. You know what a lake for food looks like: clear and deep. If you are hungry, stop to dive for food on one that looks right.

"Fly on for part of that first day and you will come to another big, long lake stretched across your path. It will be even larger than the first long lake you crossed at the beginning of the day. On this lake will be a flock of loons. Land with them and stay with them to feed and meet others. Eat plenty every day you are there. Talk and visit and learn about the next stage of the journey."

"Will you be there?" asked Chort in a very small voice.

"It depends on when you leave here," LaLa replied. "If I am, that's fine. If I'm not, that's fine too. You really don't need me any longer. You will be as big and strong as Dapper soon. Listen to the voices on the breeze and trust what they tell you. Feel the pull south in your heart and follow it."

"But, but, but…" objected Chort.

Then he went silent and thought about Dapper so big and strong and handsome, and who believed in him. He wanted to be like him. His mom always gave him good advice. He had to trust, believe, and act when the voices on the breeze spoke to him, since it seemed his mom was leaving soon too.

They stayed together on their lake for a few more days.

One day, LaLa turned to him. "Don't follow me if you see me go, Chortle. You will know your own time to leave when it comes."

"I want to go with you," Chortle complained sadly.

"I know, dear, but there's a reason you have to do this yourself, at least for the first day or two. When you find the other loons on the last big lake I told you about, then you will have more loon company. If I'm not there, other loons will tell you about the next part of the journey. Pay attention, eat, grow stronger, and wait for the breeze to whisper, 'It's time to go.' Each loon will leave when it feels right to that loon. Go when it is your time. This is the way of the loon. To do it differently would be as foolish as trying to change a loon's black and white checkers on his back."

"I don't have real checkers yet," moaned Chortle.

"All in good time, my brave little fellow," said LaLa. "Remember, I will leave and you will wait to hear the voices on the breeze telling you it's time. Then you will go. We fly south by ourselves before we are adults. I did it. Your father did it. Our parents did it. I only ask you to do what I know you can do. We have all done it since the beginning of Loon Time."

"Does that make it okay to leave me?" asked Chort.

"Of course, it does. It's the way of the loon," said his mother firmly, with pride. "You need to know you can do this. Your father and I know you can make the trip, but you must believe in yourself, and you will find your own way south. Some other birds migrate with their young ones, but you are a loon. You are not a duck or an eagle or a sparrow, or a red-winged blackbird. Each kind of bird has a different way. Be who you are and follow your own way, as it comes to you."

"All right, Mother," Chortle said sadly. "I believe you. Just don't leave when I'm looking, or I can't help it, I'll follow you."

His mother had her head tilted to one side and had a far-away look in her eye.

"What was that, dear?" she asked.

"Leave when I'm not looking so I don't follow you," said Chortle loudly. Then he dove and spent a long time chasing and eating herring. When he surfaced, LaLa had gone.

"The way of the loon," said Chortle sadly, looking around at the empty lake.

The Way of the Loon

Little loon alone and brave,
Get ready now and don't delay.
Winter comes like night descends,
But from the north with cruel revenge,
For summer days you laughed and played.
Get ready now, and don't delay.

(Voices on the breeze)

After LaLa flew away south Chortle kept on as before: swimming, diving, eating, and flying, alone. He lengthened his flights, making larger and larger circles of his lake, observing the surrounding country and neighbouring lakes. Being alone meant he made all his own decisions and he knew he must make the right ones.

He visited nearby lakes and remembered what was special about each one. There was Double Lake with its twin parts, and Big Long Lake. He knew their shapes from the air and how to return to his lake, the Round Crystal-Clear Lake. He flew farther every day, lengthening his flights to build up strength.

Days were shorter and often cooler than they had been before his mother left. One night it was clear and cold. The stars were fierce and bright and looked closer than ever before. In the morning there was a cloud of mist on the lake. He was drifting and watching the day brighten and the mist lifting as the first rays of sun hit it. As the mist rose, wafting by him, he heard a soft voice whisper, "Time to go, time to leave, time to go, time to leave."

"Right then," said Chortle, sure and strong. "I'm leaving today, but where am I going?"

A little breeze lifting the last tendrils of mist whispered to him, "When the sun is highest and warmest, fly towards it."

He waited and the day warmed. He ate his fill. He dozed. Then at the warmest part of the day, he left. He flew into the path of the sun as it glittered on the lake.

"It's the way of the loon," he told himself as he rose on his wings and flew over hills and lakes and forests, following the pull to the south. Right above the bright gold on the water, right toward the warmth of the south he flew. He didn't look back, only ahead.

THE LAST BIG LAKE

C hortle flew on. He felt the pull to the south in his chest and followed it with ease. The sun went lower to his sunset side and he flew on. He did not want to fly at night but he wanted to find the last big lake with the other loons on it, as LaLa had described to him. Then the big long lake came into view. It stretched away to his sunset side. It had many bays, but

There were many loons there.

at a wide part of the lake he spotted loons on the water. There were many, and they were a lively group, diving and popping up in the middle of the big water.

There's food there, thought Chortle, and I'm hungry and I'm tired! He flew straight in and swished to a stop right beside three other loons. There were black and white ones and even a couple of brown and white like he was. He spoke to them.

"Hi, I'm Chortle, son of Dapper and LaLa. This is my first journey south. Do you mind if I join you?"

"Not at all," answered one big male loon. "I'm Tuxedo, Tuxie for short. Any son of Dapper's is a loon I'm happy to meet."

Chortle was so pleased! He had come this far by following the pull to the south. Now he knew he was on the right path because Dapper had been here before him.

He dove and found good fish. He popped up and saw there were others all around him, diving and feeding. The evening was quiet. The air was still, the lake calm.

Mom gave me good directions, he thought, but I got here on my own!

He looked around at this new lake in the warmth of the evening light. All around him other loons were diving and rising. He felt a glow of pride in his chest that mirrored the glow of the evening light. A light breeze wisped over him, riffling the water, and he heard the soft voices on the wind whisper, "It's the way of the loon."

It made his heart swell with pride. Yes, it's the way of the loon, he thought, and I am doing it, all by myself!

Summer is Gone

Summer was gone; school had started again for the little boys in the house on the shore of the lake. They were getting ready for bed.

"There are no more loons on the lake now. Even the baby brown and white loon is gone," the older boy said.

Their mother sat down in the chair between the boys' two beds.

"Well," she said, "that fits right in with our story, which we have nearly finished."

She opened a little book called *The Way of the Loon*, read for a bit, and finished with:

On His Own

Little loon alone and brave,

Get ready now and don't delay.

Winter comes like night descends,

But from the north with cruel revenge,

For summer days you laughed and played.

Get ready now and fly away.

(Voices on the breeze)

The End

ACKNOWLEDGEMENTS

I would like to thank my brother, John Pringle, for so generously giving me the benefit of his writing experience and expertise.

As well, I would like to thank some early readers of this story, Margaret Wanlin, Julia Hedley, Pauline Tindale, and Mary and Jane Elder, for their encouragement and enthusiasm.

About The Author

Sally E. Burns has always loved lake country, and grew up in northwestern Ontario, paddling, fishing, and swimming every summer on the lakes surrounding her small town.

She graduated from the University of Toronto with a BA, and eventually returned to work and live on the edge of Quetico Provincial Park. She raised her family beside a crystal-clear lake, watching all kinds of wildlife and loons also raise their young on the water. She wrote The Way of the Loon on a screened porch of her summer cottage, and when her granddaughter was born, Sally knew she also would be raised in the outdoors and would enjoy learning about the loon families.

Sally lives in Atikokan, Ontario, and spends summers in a log cabin on the shores of Eva Lake with her golden retriever.

CPSIA information can be obtained
at www.ICGtesting.com
Printed in the USA
BVHW051057110221
599626BV00003B/7